CAUGHT FOR MILKING

Fertile First Time Bimbo

Leandra Camilli

CONTENTS

Title Page

Copyright

Chapter 1   1

Chapter 2   4

Chapter 3   8

Chapter 4   11

Chapter 5   14

Chapter 6   17

Epilogue   20

Similar Books   23

About the Author   25

CHAPTER 1

His cock was already pointing straight at my face. It was mean, big, thick, and veiny. I couldn't stop looking at it even though part of me was begging for me to do that. But it was so difficult, especially when it would be the first time that I would be enjoying some cock in my mouth.

He caught me after I got lost on this island. I didn't know what happened. One moment I was sailing and the next I was here, lying on the sand and he was pointing his dick straight at me.

Perhaps the most interesting thing about this was that he was naked. From top to bottom, I could see the perfection that highlighted his body.

I couldn't help but let my eyes wander over the man's well-built physique. His muscles rippled and bulged in all the right places, and I couldn't help but imagine trailing kisses over his broad shoulders. His defined chest begged to be touched, and I couldn't resist the urge to run my hands over it.

His narrow waist was a tantalizing contrast to the powerful muscles of his arms and legs. Every inch of him was toned and strong, from his defined biceps and triceps to his powerful thigh and calf muscles.

He had a six-pack that made my fingers ache to trace each ridge, and the way he moved was nothing short of mesmerizing. He exuded confidence in a way that made my heart race, and his posture was an open invitation for me to explore every inch of him.

His skin was smooth and clear, and his hair was perfectly groomed. The overall effect was one of raw, unbridled strength, fitness, and health that made my body come alive just looking at him.

To say that I was completely under his spell would be a huge understatement. On top of that, he was grinning. A beautiful smile that could put any person in the mood that he wanted. I was pretty sure that was one of the reasons why he was smiling so devilishly at me.

He had me exactly where he wanted.

Adding to the scalding chemistry between us, his prick was already throbbing slightly, some pre-come leaking out of the slit.

"Your name is Carla, isn't it?" He asked, not dancing around the subject. He knew that my name was that. I must have told him what my name was without realizing that I did that. Sometimes, that happened, especially when I was under the effects of Ambien. I took a pill so that I didn't have to think about all the wrong things going on in my life. Those memories rammed me with a burning intensity last night.

"It is," I responded before slowly pulling my body up. I didn't finish standing up, only staying on my knees while I noticed that his prick was still pointing straight at me. The only reason why he was doing that was that he understood that I was on the verge of shoving it right into my mouth without asking for permission.

That was how hungry I was for it.

This was a beautiful, tiny island. It was surrounded by crystal-clear turquoise waters, and the sand was as white as snow. Palm trees swayed gently in the breeze, providing the perfect amount of shade.

I was mesmerized by the vibrant coral reefs just off the shore, teeming with colorful fish and other sea creatures. The island was small enough to walk around in less than an hour, but it was also packed with so much natural beauty.

I could also hear the sound of the waves crashing against the shore. The air was filled with the sweet scent of tropical flowers and the salty sea. The island was peaceful and quiet, with only the sound of the birds and the waves to keep me company, other than this Australian guy, of course.

It was the perfect getaway if it wasn't for the fact that this man had me on his iron sights right now, and I didn't think that he was going to leave me alone anytime soon.

"I'm Mitchell," he said, holding out his hand. Wait. He was holding out his hand because he wanted me to take it or because he was going to trick me into falling into his trap? For all I knew, he could shove my head down into his dick, making me swallow everything whole.

I could already imagine the last thing happening. It would hurt me so much and my mouth would never be the same.

I still took his hand and we only shared a handshake. Okay. So that went better than I expected. He had a controlled and steady grip, not too tight and not too loose, it was just right. He looked me in the eyes, making direct contact, and maintained it throughout the handshake. It was a sign of respect and genuineness.

It was also not too fast and not too slow; it was just perfect. The whole handshake lasted just a couple of seconds, but it was enough to convey his strong presence, his assertiveness, and his goal to make me feel inferior.

In the meantime, I couldn't help but wonder what it would be like if he were exploring my body with his confident hands. Just thinking about that, my pussy was already quivering.

I remained where I was, feeling the sand against my knees. It was slightly hot and I could kind of feel it prickling my skin. It was a little uncomfortable as well, but I refrained from saying anything about that to Mitchell. If he caught a whiff of it, I didn't know what he would do.

He pulled his hand back, still holding my eyes with his gaze. When he realized that I wasn't going to say anything for the time being, he commented, "it looks like you are a good person and I'm so happy we are meeting. Now, do you want to suck me off?"

If I wanted to do that? Hell yeah. He didn't need to ask me twice.

CHAPTER 2

I licked my lips, thinking about how I was going to proceed with this. With pre-come still leaking out, there wasn't much to ponder. Act and don't dwell.

Slowly but surely, I inched my hand toward his prick. I closed my fingers around it, cherishing the skin and the flesh. It was still throbbing and I felt as if it was going to explode at any moment.

But it would be so disappointing if he were shooting his come all over me and coating my face in white without letting me get to the best part of this first.

He put his hand on mine, making me glance up. After doing that and encountering his eyes, I surmised that he was trying to reassure me. Was it working? I didn't know. All I knew was that I couldn't take my hand off his prick when it was already feeling so delicious.

I brushed my finger over the slit, catching some of the come. Coating my finger with it, I lowered my head, touching my tongue on it. The moment that happened, it was like explosions were set off in my mind. I swear, it was the most delightful salty thing that I experienced in my life.

He widened his smile. "You enjoyed that, didn't you?" He asked, but it was a question that didn't need answering. I just nodded and then proceeded to brush my finger over the slit of his gland one more time.

Right after doing that, I noticed some things changing in my body. It was growing slightly hotter and I could already feel some sweat drops forming on my skin.

And then I remembered that I didn't apply sunscreen before coming here to this island. To be honest, I didn't think that I was going to find myself stranded here, with nothing to do but to please this hot Australian with perfectly groomed hair. Did he have his own hair salon or something like that here? I could only wonder.

"It's so delicious."

"From this moment on, you are going to call me Master," he demanded. I gulped. I knew that there was no way around that. He wanted me to call him Master and that was exactly what I was going to do from this moment on.

I nodded and lowered the skin of his prick, noticing that he was uncut. A little bit more skin than I was accustomed to, the memory of my hubby striking me back. Contrasting to Mitchell here, he was circumcised. It was different for him. He wasn't as sensitive as Mitchell was.

The moment I lowered his skin a little bit, his legs already shook slightly. It was a beautiful sight to see, something that I would never forget.

My eyes couldn't help but wander over the toned, hairy legs of the man in front of me. The hair was thick and blond, covering his legs in a way that was undeniably masculine and alluring. It was well-groomed, not too much but just enough to make a statement.

I couldn't help but imagine running my hands over the rough texture of it, feeling the strength and power of his legs as I did. The muscles were toned and defined, bulging in all the right places, each one begging to be touched and explored.

It was clear that he took care of himself, that he was in great shape, and that he was confident in his own skin.

The way his hair covered his skin, the way his muscles stood out, and it was all I could obsess over. It was an experience that would be etched in my mind forever, the allure of those toned and hairy legs being so undeniable.

Following the pace of a snail, I moved my hand up and down, feeling and cherishing his skin. It was sizzling and it almost burned the skin of my hand, and I still kept on lifting and lowering my hand along his shaft.

He tilted his head back, murmuring, "yeah, like that. A little bit more of that." His words were enough to spur me on and I felt a lot more confident in what I was doing. I kept on moving my hand up and down, salivating as the seconds stretched for what felt like an eternity. It was taking everything I had not to shove his prick right into my mouth now.

I just wanted to drag this moment out for as long as possible.

After a few seconds of doing that, I noticed that Mitchell was even harder than before. He was so stiff, his dick seeming so mean, burning with his energy, that it wouldn't be surprising if this beast erupted right at this moment. But I knew that he wasn't going to do that.

Not yet, anyway.

But giving him a handjob was only going to get me so far. My hand was already hotter than it was before thanks to the friction, and that meant I had to move on to the next thing.

I stopped moving my hand up and down and Mitchell returned his gaze to me. After raising his right eyebrow, he asked, "something you want to tell me about? Why are you doing this?"

I cleared my throat, weighing the words that I was going to say, "Master, can I please suck you off?"

And upon hearing my question, we heard footsteps coming from behind me. They were confident steps coming from a person who had come here with only one goal in mind. He wanted me to please him as well.

After turning my head and seeing who it was that was coming here, I noticed that he was similar to the first Australian.

I couldn't help but be captivated by the sight of that sexy, buff Australian man in front of me. He was in his late 20s, and his rugged masculine appearance was undeniable. His skin was sun-kissed, and his chiseled jawline was something that I couldn't stop staring at.

His hair was a sandy blonde, styled in a messy yet put-together way that made me want to run my fingers through it. He had a confident and easy-going demeanor that was further accentuated by his charming Australian accent when he said, "hi there, beauty."

His physique was impressive, with a well-defined chest and broad shoulders that made my heart race. I could see his six-pack even through his clothing, and I couldn't help but imagine tracing each ridge with my fingers.

His arms were toned and strong, with biceps and triceps that were well-defined, and I couldn't help but imagine feeling the power in them. His legs were also toned and muscular, with strong thigh and calf muscles, and I couldn't help but imagine running my hands over them.

His overall appearance was one of health, fitness, and sexiness that exuded from him, and I couldn't help but feel a rush of desire in me.

He moved with grace and purpose, carrying himself with a natural confidence that was captivating. He was the type of man who turned heads wherever he went, and his charm and good looks made him impossible to ignore. I couldn't help but feel drawn to him and I also couldn't help but imagine what it would be like to be in his arms.

CHAPTER 3

"Who do we have here?" He asked after he realized that I couldn't stop mumbling, halting right behind me. Uh-oh. I didn't like his tone much. It told me he was feeling left out. In that case, I could do something about it. I could suck him off too, but only after doing the same for Mitchell and only after he told me what his name was. My mind was already begging for that.

"I'm Carla," I responded, smiling gently. He returned my smile with another smile of his, his dick pointing at me, too. Before now, it was only a semi, but now it was growing thicker and bigger as the seconds passed.

"Carla… Such a beautiful name," he murmured and as he pronounced those words, his dick grew so much thicker and fuller that now it was fully erect and pointing straight at me.

I couldn't help but lick my lips. If he were to penetrate me with that mesmerizing dick, it would be the most hurtful and pleasing experience in my life.

"I'm glad you think that," I said. This whole time, I didn't even have the opportunity to shove Mitchell's prick into my mouth. My entire body was already begging me to do that.

I returned my attention to it, this being the only thing that I could do now. Without giving it a second thought and glancing up to find the confirmation that I was seeking, I shoved his prick into my mouth. His buddy didn't even get the opportunity to tell me his name yet.

He must've noticed that about me, proceeding to tell me his

name, "I'm Jonathan, in case you are wondering," and the word was now stuck in my mind. I would never forget his name.

Mitchell's dick penetrated my mouth in a way I never thought possible. I felt it stretching and pushing my lips apart, making way. And it kept on going further inside of me. To be honest, I was probably being too hungry about this and I should take my time.

But taking my time doing this was a faraway thought in my mind right now. The only thought that was populating my mind at the moment was pleasing and worshiping his prick as much as I could. And while doing that, I also played with his balls, feeling their weight, their ruggedness, and how they were burning with desire.

I could tell that Mitchell was doing everything in his power not to come inside my mouth right now. I knew that when he was doing that, he wouldn't stop until he was filling me whole with his come. And after tasting his pre-come, I knew that the real thing had to be even tastier than the other.

It was difficult for me. I had to be swirling and moving my tongue around his gland, savoring every part of it as I focused on the underside. It was where he was most sensitive.

That also worked the way I thought it was going to. He truly was much more sensitive underside. I had some experience giving blowjobs, but this one still felt a little different from all the others I had given before.

I just kept on swirling and spreading my tongue around his gland, my hand more often than not playing with his balls, too. Now, there was no point of no return anymore and I knew that he was going to stop this only when he was shooting his load down my throat. To be honest, my mind was already begging him to do that.

I was scarcely aware of the other buff Australian standing behind me. I knew that he was jacking off slowly, preparing himself for when I was doing the same thing. They were my Masters, but I was their sole point of attention right now. If Jonathan couldn't hold on for a little while longer, I was pretty sure that he was going to shoot his come all over me, and he would only stop after emptying his nuts.

The possibility of that happening was already enticing my mind much more than I thought it could be. And I felt much more confident in the way that I was swirling and sliding my tongue around Mitchell's massive gland.

Then, I knew that he couldn't hold it any longer. I knew that he was going to erupt in me, thus it was unsurprising when it happened. He trembled and shook like a wild beast in my mouth and it was absolutely exhilarating. I couldn't stop what I was doing anymore.

The only thing that I could feel was his balls shooting out his come into my mouth and after feeling it going all the way down to my stomach, I noticed that it was changing something in me.

And whatever it was, it was making me even curvier than I already was, no exaggeration.

CHAPTER 4

I remembered feeling my breath coming in ragged gasps as I struggled to catch my breath. My chest was heaving, and my heart was pounding in my chest. I could feel the sweat on my skin, and my muscles were burning from the exertion. I closed my eyes and focused on taking deep breaths, trying to slow my breathing and calm my galloping heart.

It felt like an eternity before I finally managed to get my breathing under control. I opened my eyes and felt the cool breeze on my sweat-dampened skin; it was refreshing and invigorating. I took a moment to compose myself, feeling the rush of endorphins and the sense of accomplishment for pushing myself to my limits.

I remembered feeling the viscous, thick, white liquid on my tongue. It was slightly warm and had a distinct texture. It coated my tongue and left a slick feeling in my mouth. It was rich and creamy, with a subtle sweetness that was hard to ignore.

It was a new sensation for me and I was curious about its taste. It was a bit unusual but not unpleasant, and it was something different and exciting. I let it linger on my tongue for a moment, savoring the flavor before swallowing it.

The aftertaste was still there, no denying it. And after swallowing all the pre-come and pretty much everything else, I glanced up and found Mitchell's eyes. Mitchell was glaring back at me. The smirk on his face told me that he found what just happened to be extremely enticing. He wanted more.

My body was suddenly growing much bigger, too. It was as if

every inch of me was growing and expanding. My waistline felt wider and my hips became rounder and more pronounced, they felt heavier and curvier. I could see my hips and thighs filling out, becoming more voluptuous and womanlier. My breasts swelled, becoming fuller and heavier.

All of a sudden, I wasn't the same person anymore. I was so much more than that. I was someone else. Even opening my mouth and using it to form words were difficult things to do.

I knew that it was a desired change, but what happened exactly?

Mitchell placed his hand on my forehead, stroking my hair gently. "I guess that I should have told you before that this was going to happen. You've just transformed into a hucow, and now your only purpose is to make us more and more milk. On this island, we are kings and we can do anything we want here. You like that, don't you?"

Again, it was difficult for me to pronounce the words that were in my mind. It was as if something was closing my mouth. My lips also felt bigger and fuller, readier to give a blowjob. It was perfect, and maybe too much so.

I turned around, noticing that Jonathan was also gazing at me with only one question in mind. *Are you going to suck me off right now too or should I do something about that?* And given the way that he was glaring at me, I could tell that he wasn't at all pleased with me giving his buddy a blowjob first.

But he didn't need to feel so concerned about that. After all, I only gave Mitchell a blowjob first because he was the first one that found me.

I ran my tongue along my moist lips, preparing myself for what was going to come. But it seemed that Jonathan had other plans in mind, plans which involved him milking me for everything that I had in my udders. After all, I could already feel them growing bigger and heavier. When Mitchell said that I was going to be producing milk, he didn't lie.

Jonathan leaped, positioning himself right underneath me a moment later. He grabbed one of my udders, his fingers pressing into it with force. He wasn't hurting me, but he was applying enough strength to show me that he was the boss here and that he could control me in whatever way he saw fit.

A moment of silence, the waves crashing against the shore. He slipped my nipple into his mouth, sucking on it gently. The man knew what he was doing, his tongue already performing magic on my teat. And in return, I could only arch my back and toes.

There was nothing like what he was doing, and I could feel the pleasure that he was showering me with traversing through my entire body. It was overwhelming and I didn't know how much longer I could last. Given the look on his face, I could tell that he was extremely thirsty. He would only stop milking me when he was sated.

It seemed to be going on and on forever and I could still feel the aftertaste of Mitchell's hot come on my tongue. I didn't think that it would ever be possible for me to get rid of it. On top of that, what we were doing was far from enough for me, so I had to decide to do something else.

I decided to grab Jonathan's prick. It was under me as well and reaching it was easy. After my fingers were already closed around it, I began to pump it slowly and nicely before picking up the pace.

When I was performing the movement a lot more gracefully than before, I knew that I was only going to stop jerking him off when he was pumping his load all over my big belly.

It was so big, as if I was pregnant, even though I wasn't.

CHAPTER 5

A few minutes later and he was already emptying my udder. Seriously, I thought it was going to take him a lot longer to do that. I could feel the difference between it and the other udder, which was still full. His eyes flicking in that direction, and I knew that he was already thinking about emptying it as well.

But I didn't think that Mitchell was going to take so kindly to him doing something like that. After all, turning my head and peeking over my shoulder, I could tell that he was on the verge of orgasming for the second time today. His hand was pumping his dick viciously and he was entirely focused on that, to the point of his hand blurring and his muscles seeming more strained than before.

Following that, I wasn't surprised when he was shooting out his come in thick ropes, one after the other, all over me. It was absolutely delicious and each was hotter than the other. And there were also so many ropes of come, too. It seemed never-ending, even though it wasn't.

By the time he was done, he was panting. His chest was expanding and contracting, his muscles relaxing, though only a little. His hand, the one that he was using to jerk off, appeared to be redder than the other. I was either imagining things or he was pumping his prick so viciously that the friction almost hurt his skin.

He smiled, his eyes finding Jonathan. "Buddy, I think that I'm going to milk her other udder. One for each of us, don't you agree?"

He suggested, shuffling toward me.

The sweat glistened on his body; it was a sight that was hard to ignore. His skin was slick with it, and I could see the beads of sweat running down his chest and back. I could smell the musky scent of his sweat and it was a heady and alluring aroma.

I felt a rush of heat as I watched him, the sweat on his body making him look even more attractive and masculine. It was a sign that he had been working hard, and I couldn't help but admire his dedication and discipline. The way the sweat clung to his skin made him look even more irresistible.

Jonathan didn't seem exactly pleased by that, but he wasn't going to fight against his friend and business partner now. He slid away from me and stood up in a heartbeat. Petting my head, he told me without using words that there was much more to come.

Mitchell eased himself underneath me. I could feel the heat of his body emanating from it and it was making me sweat even more than I already was. My pussy was quivering right now, too, and I could only wonder when they were going to split it open with their thick shafts. My mind was already begging for them to do that. Without a shred of doubt, I was theirs for the rest of my life.

He brushed a finger on my nipple, making sure that the contact lasted as long as possible. Then, he eased the teat into his mouth, closing his lips around it slowly and nicely. I could feel the cozy heat coming from his mouth and it was preparing my teat for the next thing that was going to come.

He began to apply pressure with his lips. On top of that, he dropped his hand on my ass, finding my asshole. He slipped his finger inside it, and I could only arch my back. I thought that he was going to start by pleasing my cunt, but it was obvious that he had other plans in mind.

After that, the man began to move it with a circular motion, oftentimes inserting more and more of it inside of me. He knew what he was doing and he was precise in his movements.

I could feel the way that his finger was finishing circles inside my asshole, and then he put it all the way inside, forcing me to let out a moan.

He smiled after noticing that. It was exactly the kind of reaction he was expecting from me.

Mitchell then took his finger out, his lips still applying pressure on my teat. I could feel my milk coming out and going into his mouth. He was milking everything I had and by the time that he was done, I knew that my udder would be utterly empty.

A few seconds after that, I noticed Jonathan positioning himself behind me. I couldn't look over my shoulder since my body was so much bigger now, but I knew that he was planning on doing something evil to me.

His eyes had to be fixed on my moist cunt. Maybe he was already planning on splitting it open with his raging dick. And if that was the case, I was already mentally preparing myself.

"You look absolutely ready for this, Carla," he murmured before mounting me and touching the tip of his dick to my sex. I knew that we would eventually reach this point, but I didn't think that it was going to create and instigate the shockwave of pleasure that shot through my entire body.

It destroyed me completely, making me come then and there. It was like a wave washing over me, starting from my toes and working its way up my body. My legs were trembling and my core was contracting and expanding in waves.

My breath was coming in short gasps as I tried to keep up with him. My chest was heaving and my nipples were hard and sensitive to the touch. My arms were tingling, and my fingers were twitching with the desire to touch and feel.

My mind was a haze of pleasure and my body was on fire with desire. It was an intense and overwhelming feeling, and I couldn't help but let myself be swept away by it.

And to think that there were so many more moments like this to come.

CHAPTER 6

With Jonathan behind me now, there wasn't much I could do. He looked up from over me and asked, "Buddy, do you have any problems with me starting this?" And by asking that, he obviously meant splitting open my cunt. It was already begging for him to do that.

Mitchell was still milking and drinking my milk. I didn't think that he had much time to say anything about anything. He grunted something and even though he was right underneath me, I was unable to make out the words.

Jonathan smirked, moving his cock against my pussy's entrance. I could feel his fingers on my ass as though he was trying to keep me in place so that I didn't try to move away.

After all, when he was penetrating me and easing himself inside of me, I knew that he was going to create waves of pleasure inside of me. More pain than pleasure, to be more precise. I was going to be squealing like a pig, too.

Slowly but surely, he inserted his dong inside of me. I could feel it stretching my walls slowly. I could feel the pain that it was to lose my virginity. That's right. I was losing my virginity and it was going to be a memory I would never forget.

In the meantime, Mitchell was still sucking and drinking my milk. I didn't think that there was anything that could be done to change his mind about doing that. He didn't want to do anything else.

I had to be doing something as well, so I didn't refrain from finding my clit and rubbing it slowly. I was doing this slowly because I didn't want to rush anything. And, it was working as well.

With Jonathan inside of me, he found a little resistance, which was my seal of virginity, but he quickly popped it as if it was nothing. A few moments following that, he bottomed me out, and I could even feel his balls pressing against my ass.

His body was covering mine entirely and even though I was now much bigger than before, I still felt like a tiny thing that couldn't protect herself from anything. And Jonathan was as if he was growing bigger inside of me with each passing second; something I thought I would never think in all of my life.

He began to roll his hips a few moments after that. He was smiling devilishly and he knew that he had me under his full control. From that moment onward, it was only him, ramming against me with everything he had.

And the best thing about that? It was that he was going to impregnate me. I was extremely fertile and even though I couldn't be sure about this at the moment, I knew that my becoming a hucow had to be involved.

My body began to respond to the way that he was ramming in and out of me. He was relentless, his balls slapping off against my butt. And then, he jammed his prick inside of me one last time before erupting.

I could feel his prick trembling and shaking inside of me. It was almost as if it was moving and doing the things that it was doing on its own and Jonathan didn't have any more control over it. From that moment on, he spurted out rope after rope of come inside of me, filling me to the brim with it. An unforgettable memory.

He finished unloading what was in his balls and I knew for certain that I was pregnant with his heir - or maybe many heirs if I was lucky enough.

From that moment on, he stayed inside of me. Maybe he just wanted to make sure that I wasn't going to lose any of his milk. And he didn't need to worry about something like that, of course.

My pussy would never be the same, but it was still tight.

A few months after that, he pulled out of me with a moist pop sound. Then, his hands roamed and explored my ass before giving it a loud smack. I couldn't see his eyes or his face, but I could tell that he was absolutely pleased with the way this went.

In the meantime, Mitchell was already finishing up milking my other udder, which meant that now was his turn to shoot his seed inside of me. And considering that he was going to do that, I wouldn't know who was going to be the father of the babies.

To be honest, that didn't matter much right now. What mattered was giving him the experience of his life.

Having thought that, he took my teat out of his mouth before standing up with a throaty grunt. He went around me, mounted me, and in one swift movement, impaled me as if I was nothing.

He began to ram in and out of me with everything he had. His balls were already slapping against my ass, shockwaves created from it traversing over my skin before continuing from there and covering my entire body.

Sweat drops covered my entire skin. On top of that, I was also matching him thrust for thrust. His finger found my clit a few seconds after that and he didn't refrain from scratching it.

Those things combined were enough to bring me over the edge and I came at the same time as he did. My body shook with pleasure, sweat drops jumping off of it and wetting the sand underneath me.

By the time he was done with me and so was his buddy, I was still trying to catch my breath, but it was okay. After dicking around with my husband, I had a molded and unchangeable realization in my mind.

I had found my true calling.

EPILOGUE

But finding my true calling didn't mean that things were going to be easy. Or they were going to be, somewhat. I was lying on a small boat, the waves making it rock comfortably. I wasn't far from the island, of course, and Mitchell and Jonathan were also here with me.

Their hands were still exploring every inch of my body, and it felt like they couldn't stop doing that even if they wanted to.

Their digitals were obsessed with my belly. The look of pride on their faces was undeniable. They knew that I was going to give them heirs.

Gosh, the population on this island was going to explode, considering that it was going to jump thanks to the other hucows, who were also going to give them more heirs.

And then, world domination would only be the start. I giggled at that thought.

Someone's finger found my weak spot. My cunt. He slipped his finger in there, turning it and rotating it until he found my g-spot. After that, he continued to give it a few strokes, driving me crazy. My moans could be heard all the way from the island, most likely making the other hucows envious of me.

But I wasn't thinking so much about them at the moment. At the moment, my hand was roaming over my big belly. It had grown so much bigger since they knocked me up, and I was pretty certain that it was still going to grow even bigger in the coming months.

I couldn't even open my eyes. I didn't want to find out who had his finger inside my cunt at the moment. Still… I did that a few moments after that, realizing that the one that was doing that was none other than Mitchell.

The smile on his face was telling me everything he was thinking. He was absolutely obsessed with me and he knew that after I delivered his heirs, he was going to lock me up one more time alongside his buddy.

I could barely wait for that, to be honest. And just when I thought I was going to get some reprieve, Jonathan eased his finger into my sex, replacing his buddy's.

He began to play with it, finding my g-spot a few moments after that. And then he made me come, my body trembling with everything it had. Honestly, I didn't think that it was going to be such a powerful climax.

By the time it was over, my chest was rising and contracting. I had a beautiful smile on my face that told the Australians everything they needed to know about what I was thinking right now.

From this moment on, I was their property much more than ever before.

End of Book 3

My top series starters:

1. Hucow Flavor
2. Cowboys' Lucky Age Gap
3. Condemned to the Hucow Prison
4. Leaky Bimbo
5. Peculiar Dairy

Thank you for reading this story. Leave your review. Your

feedback helps me immensely!

SIMILAR BOOKS

SERIES - Hucow for White Collars

1. Milked by Lawyers

2. Milked by Doctors

3. Milked by Engineers

4. Milked by Directors

5. Milked by Managers

SERIES - Fertile Only

1. Bumping the Teacher

2. Bumping the Midwife

3. Bumping the Farmhand

4. Bumping the Sinner

SERIES - Mafia Cowboys

1. Fertile for the Cocky Italians

2. Tied Up for the Cocky Italians

3. Serving the Cocky Italians

SERIES - Historical Hucows

1. Milked by Cavemen

2. Milked by Dukes

3. Milked by WW2 Soldiers

4. Milked by Kings

5. Milked by Princes

SERIES - Hucow for Blue Collars

1. Milked by Plumbers

2. Milked by Firefighters

3. Milked by Policemen

4. Milked by Electricians

5. Milked by Miners

SERIES - Welcome to my Harem

Joining his harem means obeying all of his rules. How much do they want his *big surprise*?

1. Bimbo Magic

2. When he Creams

3. Christmas Comes

4. Christmas Cream

5. Holiday Milking

6. Don't Pull Out

ABOUT THE AUTHOR

Leandra Camilli is an author who is passionate about writing dirty, steamy stories that captivate her readers. She loves to pitch hucows with burly, Alpha males, but she also has a huge collection featuring all kinds of other genres. If you're looking for this type of literature, you won't be disappointed with her offerings.

Leandra is known for her commitment to her craft and can often be found at her writing desk with a cup of coffee and a pair of warm socks on her feet. She writes almost every day and has been fortunate enough to be featured in several top 100 categories in the store. Despite her success, she remains humble and continues to publish new stories weekly for her devoted readers.

9 798374 967746